MR. COOL

by Roger Hargreaves

TO:

_____

FROM:

_____

EAN

ISBN 978-0-8431-3351-6

9 780843 133516

5 0 3 9 9 >

MR. COOL

Roger Hargreaves

Written and illustrated by Adam Hargreaves

PSS!
PRICE STERN SLOAN
An Imprint of Penguin Group (USA) Inc.

Poor Jack Robinson wasn't feeling very well.

He had been in bed for days and he had to stay in bed until he was better.

"I'm bored," he huffed. "I wish I could go outside and play with my friends."

Suddenly, a blue blur shot in through the open window.

It looped-the-loop around the light on the ceiling, and a small blue figure wearing a hat landed on the end of Jack's bed.

"Cool!" said Jack.

"That's me. Mr. Cool," said Mr. Cool.

"Cool!" repeated Jack.

"You look a bit bored," said Mr. Cool. "I thought we could go and have some fun."

"I wish I could," said Jack, "but I'm not allowed out of bed."

"I think we could make an exception just this once," said Mr. Cool, and he snapped his fingers.

The next instant, Jack found himself sitting in the cockpit of an airplane.

"Why don't you take it out for a spin?" suggested Mr. Cool.

"What? Can I really fly it?" said Jack.

"Sure you can," said Mr. Cool. "It's easy!"

So Jack flew the plane out across the Atlantic Ocean and back.

"That was cool," cried Jack when they were back on the ground. "Thanks, Mr. Cool!"

"We haven't finished yet," said Mr. Cool, and he snapped his fingers again.

Jack heard a crowd roar. He was at a soccer game, but he wasn't sitting in the crowd. He was on the bench with the other players!

And he was even wearing the team uniform!

"Quick!" said Mr. Cool. "The manager wants you to play."

"He wants me to play?" said Jack incredulously. "But they're a major league team!"

And you'll never guess what . . . Jack scored the winning goal!

"Wow! That was so cool!" said Jack.

As Jack walked off the field, Mr. Cool snapped his fingers and whisked them away.

To climb the tallest tree in the world!

He snapped his fingers again and before you could say Jack Robinson . . .

. . . they were standing on top of a mountain!

"Where are we?" called Jack over the noise of the wind.

"Mount Everest!" said Mr. Cool.

"How cool! What are we doing here?" shouted Jack.

"Sledding!" said Mr. Cool. "Let's go!"

Jack and Mr. Cool slid from the very top to the very bottom of Mount Everest.

"That was the coolest thing ever!" cried Jack.

"It was more like the c . . . c . . . coldest," stuttered Mr. Cool.

For the final time that day, Mr. Cool snapped his fingers.

In an instant, Jack found himself back in his bedroom.

"Thank you so much, Mr. Cool," said Jack. "That was . . ."

". . . amazing?!" laughed Mr. Cool.

"Well, I'll be off," said Mr. Cool. "But there's one more thing, Jack. Take a look in the mirror."

With that, Mr. Cool shot out through the open window.

Jack went into the bathroom and looked in the mirror.

"Cool!" said Jack when he saw himself.

And why do you think Jack was so pleased?

That's right, all his spots had disappeared. Jack was better.

I wonder, on which page did Jack get better?

Mr. Cool™ and copyright © 2003 by THOIP (a Chorion company). All rights reserved
worldwide. First published in the United States in 2008 by Price Stern Sloan, a division
of Penguin Young Readers Group, 345 Hudson Street, New York, New York 10014.
PSS! is a registered trademark of Penguin Group (USA) Inc. Printed in the U.S.A.

www.ilovemrmen.com

The publisher does not have any control over and does not assume
any responsibility for author or third-party websites or their content.

ISBN 978-0-8431-3351-6   10 9 8 7 6 5 4 3

MR. MEN   LITTLE MISS

PSS!
PRICE STERN SLOAN

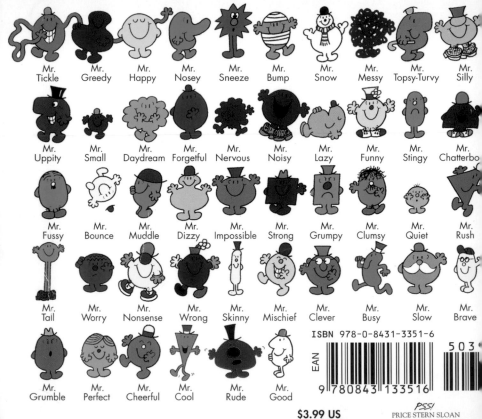

Mr. Tickle · Mr. Greedy · Mr. Happy · Mr. Nosey · Mr. Sneeze · Mr. Bump · Mr. Snow · Mr. Messy · Mr. Topsy-Turvy · Mr. Silly

Mr. Uppity · Mr. Small · Mr. Daydream · Mr. Forgetful · Mr. Nervous · Mr. Noisy · Mr. Lazy · Mr. Funny · Mr. Stingy · Mr. Chatterbox

Mr. Fussy · Mr. Bounce · Mr. Muddle · Mr. Dizzy · Mr. Impossible · Mr. Strong · Mr. Grumpy · Mr. Clumsy · Mr. Quiet · Mr. Rush

Mr. Tall · Mr. Worry · Mr. Nonsense · Mr. Wrong · Mr. Skinny · Mr. Mischief · Mr. Clever · Mr. Busy · Mr. Slow · Mr. Brave

Mr. Grumble · Mr. Perfect · Mr. Cheerful · Mr. Cool · Mr. Rude · Mr. Good

ISBN 978-0-8431-3351-6

EAN

503

9 780843 133516

$3.99 US
($4.99 CAN)

PSS!
PRICE STERN SLOAN

www.penguin.com/youngrea